Hangdog

Graham Round

Beaver Books

To Kate, Melissa, and Josh

A Beaver Book
Published by Arrow Books Limited
62-5 Chandos Place, London WC2N 4NW
An imprint of Century Hutchinson Ltd

London Melbourne Sydney Auckland
Johannesburg and agencies throughout the world

First published by Hutchinson Children's Books 1987

Beaver edition 1988

© Graham Round 1987

Printed and bound in Great Britain
by Scotprint, Musselburgh, Scotland

ISBN 0 09 956790 3

Hangdog was the loneliest dog in the world.

Although he was gentle and kind and very polite, he just couldn't seem to make friends however hard he tried.

Just one friend would do, Hangdog often thought; someone to come to tea. Every day he got out his best china and set the table for two. But no one ever came.

Sometimes he would stand in front of the mirror and try to work out what was wrong. 'Maybe it's my growly voice,' he said. 'Or maybe I'm too fat. Or perhaps my face is too sad.' But in the end he had to admit he was just a plain old hangdog that nobody liked.

One day it rained and rained. The city was dark and cold and full of puddles. Hangdog put on his raincoat and wandered down to the docks. As he looked out to sea he felt lonelier than ever.

Watching the boats bob about on the waves gave Hangdog an idea. 'I'll build myself a boat and sail away to sea,' he said. 'There *must* be a friend for me somewhere in the world.'

Back at home, Hangdog searched for something that would make a boat.
In the corner of the shed stood an old grandfather clock.

He pulled it down from its dusty corner. The insides had all gone, but it had a happy face with a big smile.

'A grandfather boat,' said Hangdog. 'Perfect!'

A broomstick made a very good mast. An old tablecloth made a sail.
A coal shovel made an excellent rudder.

Hangdog collected all the things he would need for his journey:
some tins of marrowbone jelly, a rubber bone, a compass, a pair of
binoculars and an umbrella in case it rained.

At last the boat was ready. Hangdog trundled it down to the shore.

No one noticed as the wind took up the tablecloth sail and blew the little grandfather boat out to sea.

A whole day passed. Soon, Hangdog could see nothing but sea for miles and miles. He sniffed the salty air. He was all alone, but he didn't feel lonely at all.

That night, the sky grew dark and stormy. It began to rain and the waves rocked the little boat to and fro. This *is* exciting, thought Hangdog.

But as the night wore on the storm grew worse; the waves grew bigger
and bigger and the wind grew stronger and stronger. A huge wave
swept Hangdog overboard.

All night long, Hangdog hung bravely on to the mast. At last the storm passed and morning came. Hangdog looked around him, but there was no sign of the little grandfather boat.

Suddenly, a huge jet of water shot into the air.
   What now, thought Hangdog.

A great whale rose out of the water. It opened its enormous mouth.
  'Hello,' said Hangdog. But just like everyone else, the whale didn't even notice him.

Hangdog swam on. Soon a faint outline appeared on the horizon.
Was that land ahead?

It was. Hangdog doggy-paddled furiously, and soon he reached the shore of a desert island. He was so tired he lay down and fell asleep. All night long he slept on the sand, dreaming of storms and waves and boats and whales.

The next morning he awoke with a start and decided at once to explore.
He walked up the beach and into a strange jungle world. He had never
seen anything like it before.

As he wandered deeper and deeper into the jungle he had the curious feeling that he was being watched.

Suddenly, a huge tiger leapt out of the bushes.
   'Oh, dear,' cried Hangdog. He turned and ran, and with a great roar the tiger came after him.

Tiger chased Hangdog. What a chase! Hangdog ran and ran and ran until he came to a clearing. He looked right and he looked left, but there was nowhere else to run.

The tiger flashed out of the trees.

'Oh well,' said Hangdog, 'you may as well eat me. No one will miss me and no one will care.'

Drooling at the mouth, the huge tiger looked at Hangdog.

Then he gave Hangdog a great big slobbery kiss!

'Eat you!' he said. 'Not likely! I've been so lonely here on my own, I've been waiting for a friend just like you.' And Tiger hugged Hangdog as if he would never let him go.

'I *knew* there was a friend for me somewhere in the world,' said Hangdog. And that night Tiger got out his very best china and the two friends took tea together under the moon.

Other titles in the Beaver/Sparrow Picture Book series:

An American Tail

The Bad Babies Counting Book Tony Bradman and Debbie van der Beek

Bear Goes to Town Anthony Browne

The Big Sneeze Ruth Brown

Crazy Charlie Ruth Brown

The Grizzly Revenge Ruth Brown

If At First You Do Not See Ruth Brown

Our Cat Flossie Ruth Brown

Harriet and William and the Terrible Creature Valerie Carey and Lynne Cherry

In the Attic Hiawyn Oram and Satoshi Kitamura

Ned and the Joybaloo Hiawyn Oram and Satoshi Kitamura

What's Inside? Satoshi Kitamura

The Adventures of King Rollo David McKee

The Further Adventures of King Rollo David McKee

The Hill and the Rock David McKee

I Hate My Teddy Bear David McKee

King Rollo's Letter and Other Stories David McKee

King Rollo's Playroom David McKee

Not Now Bernard David McKee

Two Can Toucan David McKee

Two Monsters David McKee

Tusk Tusk David McKee

The Truffle Hunter Inga Moore

The Vegetable Thieves Inga Moore

Babylon Jill Paton Walsh and Jennifer Northway

Robbery at Foxwood Cynthia and Brian Paterson

The Foxwood Treasure Cynthia and Brian Paterson

The Foxwood Regatta Cynthia and Brian Paterson

The Foxwood Kidnap Cynthia and Brian Paterson

The Tiger Who Lost His Stripes Anthony Paul and Michael Foreman

The Magic Pasta Pot Tomie de Paola

Mary Had a Little Lamb Tomie de Paola

We Can Say No! David Pithers and Sarah Greene

The Boy Who Cried Wolf Tony Ross

Goldilocks and the Three Bears Tony Ross

The Three Pigs Tony Ross

Terrible Tuesday Hazel Townson and Tony Ross

There's A Crocodile Under My Bed Dieter and Ingrid Schubert

Emergency Mouse Bernard Stone and Ralph Steadman

Inspector Mouse Bernard Stone and Ralph Steadman

Quasimodo Mouse Bernard Stone and Ralph Steadman

The Fox and the Cat Kevin Crossley-Holland and Susan Varley

Crocodile Teeth Marjorie Ann Watts

The Tale of Fearsome Fritz Jeanne Willis and Margaret Chamberlain

The Tale of Mucky Mabel Jeanne Willis and Margaret Chamberlain